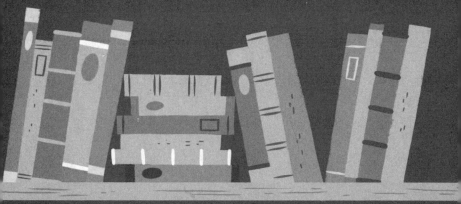

The HAUNTED LIBRARY

FOR MY MOM
—DHB

* * * * * * * * * * * * * * * * * *

GROSSET & DUNLAP
Penguin Young Readers Group
An Imprint of Penguin Random House LLC

Penguin supports copyright. Copyright fuels creativity, encourages diverse voices, promotes free speech, and creates a vibrant culture. Thank you for buying an authorized edition of this book and for complying with copyright laws by not reproducing, scanning, or distributing any part of it in any form without permission. You are supporting writers and allowing Penguin to continue to publish books for every reader.

Text copyright © 2016 by Dori Hillestad Butler. Illustrations copyright © 2016 by Aurore Damant. All rights reserved. Published by Grosset & Dunlap, an imprint of Penguin Random House LLC, 345 Hudson Street, New York, New York 10014. GROSSET & DUNLAP is a trademark of Penguin Random House LLC. Printed in the USA.

Library of Congress Cataloging-in-Publication Data is available.

ISBN 9780448489421 (pbk)   10 9 8 7 6 5 4 3 2 1
ISBN 9780448489438 (hc)   10 9 8 7 6 5 4 3 2 1

GHOSTLY GLOSSARY

EXPAND
When ghosts make themselves larger

GLOW
What ghosts do so humans can see them

HAUNT
Where ghosts live

PASS THROUGH
When ghosts travel through walls, doors, and other solid objects

SHRINK
When ghosts make themselves smaller

SKIZZY
When ghosts feel sick to their stomachs

SOLIDS
What ghosts call humans

SPEW
Ghostly vomit

SWIM
When ghosts move freely through the air

TRANSFORMATION
When a ghost takes a solid object and turns it into a ghostly object

WAIL
What ghosts do so humans can hear them

The HAUNTED LIBRARY

THE HIDE-AND-SEEK GHOST

BY DORI HILLESTAD BUTLER

ILLUSTRATED BY AURORE DAMANT

GROSSET & DUNLAP * AN IMPRINT OF PENGUIN RANDOM HOUSE

CHAPTER 1

WHAT'S WITH MOM AND BECKETT?

One . . . two . . . three . . . GLOW!"
Little John shouted.

It was nighttime, and all the solid people who lived above the library were asleep. Kaz hovered in the library entryway with his mom, pops, and little brother. They were all glowing.

Kaz scrunched up his face. He gritted his teeth. He squeezed his hands into tight fists. And he tried, tried, *tried* to glow like the rest of his family. But no matter what

he did, no matter how hard he tried, Kaz couldn't glow.

"I know you can do this," Mom told Kaz as the glow faded from her body.

"You've mastered all your other ghost skills," Pops said.

It was true. Kaz could wail now. He could also pass through solid walls and pick up solid objects. He could even transform solid objects into ghostly objects.

Back when he and his family lived in the old schoolhouse, Kaz couldn't do any of those things. He could only shrink and expand.

So much had happened since then.

Kaz remembered how he and his brothers used to swim around the old schoolhouse. His big brother, Finn, liked to scare Kaz and Little John by sticking an arm or a leg through the Outside wall. But

one day Finn stuck his head a little too far through the wall, and the wind pulled him all the way into the Outside. Grandmom and Grandpop tried to rescue him, but they couldn't. The wind blew them all away.

After that, Mom and Pops tried even harder to teach Kaz his ghost skills. But before Kaz had learned any new skills, the old schoolhouse was torn down. Kaz and the rest of his family ended up in the Outside, and they all got separated in the wind.

The wind blew Kaz to the library, where he met Beckett, the other ghost who lived there, and Claire. Claire was a solid girl, just Kaz's age. She could see ghosts when they weren't glowing, and she could hear ghosts when they weren't wailing. No one knew why.

Claire and Kaz started a detective

agency to solve ghostly mysteries and try to find Kaz's missing family. They'd found Kaz's parents last week. Now Finn was the only one left to find. Kaz was worried he'd never see Finn again.

"It's getting light outside," Pops said now. "It won't be long before Claire wakes up. Try again, son."

"This time don't squeeze your hands together," Mom suggested. "And don't grit your teeth. It's hard to glow when you're all tensed up. Let the glow flow through your skin."

"I don't know what that means," Kaz said.

"You don't know what *what* means?" Beckett asked as he wafted into the entryway. "Oh!" he said when he saw Kaz's mom. "I'm sorry. I didn't know you were in here."

"It's okay," Mom said tightly. Now she was the one who was all tensed up.

Kaz and Little John had hardly seen Beckett since their parents had come to the library. For some reason, Beckett and Mom didn't like to be around each other.

"We're trying to teach Kaz how to glow," Little John told Beckett. "Maybe you can help?"

Beckett shook his head. "I don't think so." He turned to leave.

"Why not?" Kaz asked. Before Kaz's parents had arrived, Beckett used to work with Kaz on his ghost skills all the time.

But Beckett wafted away without answering.

Kaz turned to his mom. "Why don't you and Beckett like each other?" he asked.

"What are you talking about?" Mom

asked, not quite meeting Kaz's gaze. "Beckett and I like each other just fine."

"It doesn't seem like it," Little John said.

"You never want to be in the same room together," Kaz pointed out.

"How *do* you two know each other, anyway?" Pops asked.

Mom shrugged like it was no big deal. "We spent some time together when we were kids."

"And . . . ?" Little John waved his hand for Mom to go on.

"And nothing," Mom said. "It was a long time ago."

Kaz could tell there was more to the story than that. What would it take to get Mom or Beckett to tell the rest of the story?

* * * * * * * * * * * * * *

"Are you ghosts ready to go to Valley View?" Claire asked later that afternoon. It was Sunday and she had promised to take Kaz, Little John, and their parents to visit Grandmom and Grandpop at the nursing home. Mom and Pops hadn't seen Grandmom and Grandpop in so long.

Woof! Woof! Cosmo barked.

"Okay, Cosmo," Kaz said, grabbing his dog around the middle. "You can come, too."

The whole family shrank down . . . down . . . down . . . and swam into Claire's water bottle. It was a tight squeeze.

Claire flung the strap from the bottle over her shoulder and called to her family, "I'm going to visit people at Valley View!"

"That's nice, honey," Grandma Karen called back. "Be back in time for dinner."

Claire walked down the street, her

water bottle swinging over her shoulder. She stopped for a red light near the fire station.

"Hey, remember when we got to see the fire trucks, Kaz?" Little John asked, glancing over at the fire station. Unfortunately, the big fire doors were closed, so Little John couldn't see the trucks inside.

"Yes," Kaz said. "I also remember that you got lost inside one of those trucks for a while."

"You did?" Mom's eyebrows shot up.

"I wasn't really lost," Little John said. "I knew where I was."

"Yeah, but *I* didn't know where you were," Kaz said. "Just like when we were looking for the five o'clock ghost and you went inside that house and didn't come out." That was the first case Little John had helped Kaz and Claire solve.

"It's good that you thought I was lost that day because that made you pass through the wall to come find me," Little John said.

Kaz couldn't argue with that. For a long time, he didn't like passing through walls. It made him feel all skizzy inside. But the more Kaz did it, the easier it got.

"It sounds like you boys have had

a lot of adventures since we've been apart," Mom said as Claire turned onto Forest Street.

"We have," Kaz agreed. He turned all around inside Claire's water bottle. "In fact, this is where I first saw Cosmo. Claire and I were inside that house over there." He pointed. "The lady who lives there thought she had a ghost in her attic, so she hired us to come find it. I looked out her window and that's when I saw Cosmo. He was right here. Right where we are now. Except he wasn't in a water bottle. He was just floating around in the Outside."

Woof! Woof! Cosmo barked, his tail wagging.

"I think he remembers!" Little John said.

"How did you ever catch him?" Mom asked.

But before Kaz could answer, a voice yelled from the window next door, "Hey! Hey, you! You're that girl who solves ghostly mysteries, aren't you? Come here! I've got a case for you."

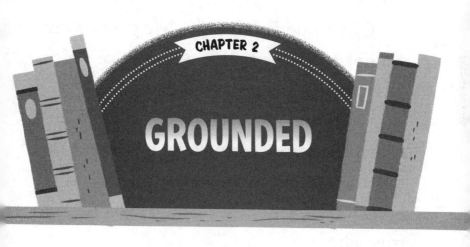

CHAPTER 2

GROUNDED

Oh no," Kaz said. He recognized that boy in the window.

"What? Who is that?" Little John asked. He, Mom, and Pops all craned their necks to see around Cosmo and the stars on Claire's water bottle.

"You don't know him," Kaz said. "But Claire and I do. His name is Eli, and he likes to play tricks on people. When we were trying to find the ghost in Mrs. Beesley's attic, we thought *he* was the ghost. Remember, Claire?"

Claire nodded slightly. "He goes to my school, too," she said in a low voice. "He's always in trouble for something."

"Why are you just standing there?" Eli called to Claire. "Come over here so I can talk to you." He waved his arm.

"Don't, Claire," Kaz said. He didn't trust Eli.

"He might have a case for us," Claire said. "I think we should find out." She adjusted the strap on her water bottle and marched over to Eli's house.

Kaz groaned.

"Don't be such a scaredy-ghost, Kaz," Little John said.

"I'm not a scaredy-ghost. I just—whoa!" Kaz shrieked as Cosmo suddenly bolted from his grasp. The dog was halfway through the bottle before Kaz and his parents managed to pull him back in.

Woof! Woof!

"No, Cosmo!" Kaz said, holding tight to his dog.

Claire stopped right below Eli's window. "Okay, I'm here," she said, shading her eyes. "What do you want to talk to me about?"

"I told you. I have a case for you," Eli said, leaning out the window. "A *ghost* case."

Woof! Woof! Cosmo wiggled and squirmed in Kaz's arms.

"Help! He's still trying to escape!" Kaz exclaimed.

It took the entire ghost family to hold Cosmo inside the water bottle.

Claire planted a hand on her hip. "I thought you didn't believe in ghosts," she said to Eli. "That's what you said when I told you that Mrs. Beesley hired me to find a ghost in her house. You even laughed at me when I said it."

Eli scratched his head. "Yeah, well, that was before a ghost moved into *my* house," he said.

"What makes you think there's a ghost in your house?" Claire asked.

"I saw it," Eli said.

"So, it was glowing," Little John said.

"If it was a real ghost," Kaz said, clinging to his dog. He knew Eli couldn't see ghosts like Claire could.

Claire unzipped her backpack and pulled out her ghost book and pen. "Can you describe it?" she asked.

Woof! Woof! Woof!

"I don't know," Eli said. "It looked like a ghost."

"What was it doing?" Claire asked.

"Hiding," Eli said. "I saw it go under my sister's bed once. I also saw it walk through a wall. And last night it hid in my closet and yelled, 'Boo!' when I opened the door."

"Ghosts don't hide from solids," Pops said with a scowl.

Kaz cringed when Pops said "solids." He knew Claire didn't like that word.

"We don't have to hide," Pops said. "If we don't want solids to see us, we simply don't glow."

"Whenever I try and follow the ghost or tell someone in my family about it, it disappears," Eli told Claire. "And then later it reappears someplace else. I think it likes to play hide-and-seek."

"Uh-huh," Claire said as she wrote down everything Eli said.

"I'm not the only one who's seen it," Eli said. "Our house is for sale. Almost everyone who has come to look at our house has seen it, too. That's why no one wants to buy our house. They think it's haunted. But no one else in my family has seen it."

Honk! Honk! A car pulled into the driveway behind Claire.

"Oh no," Eli said. "That's my mom. She and my sister are home!" He slammed his window shut and darted away.

Claire stepped onto the grass so Eli's mom could pull all the way into the driveway. She was still writing in her notebook when Eli's mom and sister got out of the car. The sister

looked a little older than Claire and Kaz.

Cosmo turned to them and wagged his tail. For some reason, he seemed a lot calmer now.

Eli's mom gave Claire a half smile, then raised her eyes to the window. "Eli," she called.

When Eli didn't appear at the window,

she cupped her hands around her mouth and shouted, "Eli!"

"Someone's in *trouuuuble,*" his sister sang.

Eli slowly returned to the window. His mom motioned for him to open it. "What does *grounded* mean?" she asked once the window was open.

Eli lowered his eyes. "It means I can't go anywhere. I can't use the computer. And I can't text," he grumbled.

"It also means you're not supposed to talk to your friends out the window." His mom gave Claire a hard look.

"I wouldn't call us Eli's friends," Kaz said. Not that Eli's mom could see or hear him.

"I'm sorry," Claire said as she stuffed her notebook back inside her backpack. "I was just walking by and—"

"Let me guess," Eli's sister interrupted. "You're that girl who finds ghosts. Eli said he was going to call you." She leaned closer to Claire. "You do know my brother likes to prank people, don't you?"

"It's not a prank, Lauren!" Eli hollered out the window.

Eli's mom put her arm around Claire and led her over to the sidewalk. "I don't know why you're here, but Eli's grounded. He can't see you today. And I assure you, there are no ghosts in our house."

Just then, Kaz caught a glimpse of something darting across the window next to Eli's. Something *ghostly*.

Kaz blinked. "Did you see that?" he asked his family.

"See what?" Little John asked.

"I don't see anything," Kaz's mom said.

"Neither do I," Pops said.

Kaz kept his eyes peeled to that window. But whatever he had seen didn't come back.

Eli's mom was still talking to Claire. "You may have noticed the For Sale sign in our yard," she said. "Eli is unhappy that we're moving, so he's been trying to trick people into believing our house is haunted."

"I am not!" Eli banged his fist against the window frame.

"He thinks that if we don't sell the house, we won't move," Lauren said.

"We *do* have a ghost in our house, Claire," Eli cried. "We really, really do!"

"Well, there's nothing I can do about it today," Claire told him. "Your mom says you're grounded. I'll see you at school tomorrow." She waved to Eli and headed down the street.

What were you talking about when you said, 'Did you see that?'" Little John asked Kaz as they floated inside Claire's water bottle. They were almost to Valley View.

Kaz held tight to Cosmo. "I thought I saw a ghost in the window next to Eli's," he explained. "I only saw it for a second, so maybe I imagined it."

"Maybe you saw the sun reflecting against the window," Mom suggested.

"Lots of things look like ghosts from a distance, but they turn out to be something else," Pops added.

Kaz knew Pops was right. He and Claire had been called to solve quite a few ghostly mysteries, but none of them had resulted in any real ghosts.

"It *could* be a ghost," Little John said. "We're not the only ghosts around here, you know. There's Beckett, there's the family that lives in the purple house, and there are a bunch of old lady ghosts at Valley View."

"Don't call them old ladies," Mom scolded. "That's not polite."

"But they *are* old ladies," Little John said. "Everyone at Valley View is old."

"We're here," Kaz announced as Claire walked up to a small brick building. She pulled open the door, and a large colorful

bird in the entryway squawked, "Hello! Hello!"

"*Ack!*" Kaz shrieked, even though the bird was in a cage.

Grrrrr! Cosmo bared his teeth and growled at the bird.

"What in the world is that?" Mom asked.

Little John giggled. "It's a bird. His name is Petey. Right, Kaz?" Little John glanced at Kaz, then looked again. "Kaz? Are you glowing?"

"You *are* glowing!" Pops exclaimed.

"I am?" Kaz looked down at himself. There was a slight bluish glow to his skin. Unfortunately, he had no idea what he was doing to make it happen.

"Wow, Kaz!" Claire said, impressed.

"Excuse me? Can I help you?" the lady at the counter asked.

Claire quickly shoved her water bottle

behind her back. "I'd uh . . . like to visit some people who live here," she said.

"*Awww,*" Kaz groaned, turning his arm all around. "The glow is gone already."

As soon as Kaz let go of Cosmo, the dog charged through Claire's water bottle—and into Petey's cage!

"Cosmo! No! BAD DOG!" Kaz yelled. He swam after his dog. While Cosmo chased Petey, Kaz chased Cosmo. Up, down, and all around the cage.

"BAD DOG! BAD DOG!" Petey squawked.

Mom, Pops, and Little John swam into the cage and tried to help Kaz catch Cosmo. But Petey flew right through them. "BAD DOG!" he squawked again.

"My goodness!" The lady at the counter rose to her feet. She couldn't see all the ghosts in the birdcage. She could

only see Petey. "I don't know what's wrong with that bird."

Claire pressed her lips together. She knew what was wrong, but there was nothing she could do to help.

"Got him!" Little John shouted as he grabbed Cosmo around the middle and swam back through the cage. Kaz and his parents followed Little John and Cosmo over to a far corner of the room—as far from Petey as they could get.

Petey shook his feathers, then uttered one more "BAD DOG!"

Once the bird was calm, the lady at the counter sat back down. "Sorry about that," she said to Claire. "Now, was there someone in particular you wanted to visit?"

"Uh." Claire thought for a second, then said, "Yes! I'd like to visit Victor Helsing!" Victor had done some repair work at the library a long time ago—long before Claire was even born. Claire, Kaz, and Little John had gone to see him when they wanted to learn more about the secret room. That was when they'd found out that Grandmom and Grandpop had made Valley View their new haunt.

"I'm sure Victor would love some company," the lady said. "He's in room 105." She wrote it on a scrap of paper and slid the paper across the counter.

Claire grabbed it. "Thanks," she said as she headed down the hall. Kaz and his family wafted behind her.

Claire stopped in the doorway of room 105. "This is Victor's room," she told the ghosts. "Come find me when you're done, or I'll come find you when I'm done."

"Okay," Kaz said. He turned to his family. "Come on. Grandmom and Grandpop are probably in the activity room."

The ghosts continued down the hall toward a large, open room. Two solid ladies and two solid men were playing a card game at a table in the middle of the room. Grandmom, Grandpop, and four other ghost ladies hovered around them.

"Hi, Grandmom! Hi, Grandpop!" Little John zoomed ahead of Kaz. "Look who we brought to visit you!"

All the ghost people *and* the solid people turned.

"Oh my!" Grandmom exclaimed.

"I didn't think we'd ever see you folks again," Grandpop said. He and Grandmom swam over and hugged Mom and Pops.

"And you brought Cosmo, too. Good to see you, old boy!" Grandpop said, giving the ghost dog a pat on the head.

Cosmo licked Grandpop's hand. Then he turned and licked Grandmom's cheek.

A solid lady with blue hair adjusted her glasses. "How nice that you're all together again!"

Pops tilted his head. "Can you see us?" he asked the solid ladies.

"Of course," one of them replied.

"Most of the solid people here can see us," Little John said.

"Really?" Mom asked.

"Don't worry, dear," Grandmom said. "Everyone here is very friendly."

"B-but they're solid!" Mom cried.

"Yes," Grandpop said, patting Mom's arm. "Believe it or not, most solids are

really very lovely people once you get to know them."

Mom and Pops both raised their eyebrows. They hadn't spent much time with solid people. Not like Kaz and Little John. And Grandmom and Grandpop.

For the next half hour, the family shared stories about everything they'd seen and done in the months they'd been apart. Time passed so quickly that they were surprised when Claire walked into the activity room. "Are you ghosts ready to go?" she asked.

"So soon?" Grandmom asked.

"You just got here," Grandpop said. "Why don't you stay awhile?"

"Yes. Stay," Grandmom said. "Valley View is a fine haunt. And we're family! Family should be together."

"Yes, family *should* be together," Mom agreed. She folded her arms. "So why are you two living here when your grandsons are living in the library?"

Uh-oh. Kaz was afraid Mom would bring that up. Were Grandmom and Grandpop in trouble?

"Don't be angry, dear," Grandmom said. "Kaz and Little John wanted to be with people their age. And we wanted to be with people our age."

Grandpop nodded. "They said they had a responsible adult ghost looking after them in the library."

"A responsible adult ghost?" Mom's voice rose. "Do you know who—"

"I hate to interrupt," Claire said, stepping in between Mom and Grandpop. "But it's almost dinnertime. I have to go home. Who's coming with me?"

"We are," Kaz said, grabbing his dog. He turned to his grandparents. "Why don't you come, too? Just for a visit."

"Yes, I think you should come to the library," Mom said.

"You've never visited us," Little John said. "But we've visited you several times."

"The boy's right," Grandmom said to Grandpop.

"Okay," Grandpop said. "We'll come."

"Hooray!" Kaz and Little John raised their fists in the air.

"You have to shrink," Little John told

his grandparents as he shrank down . . . down . . . down and swam into Claire's water bottle. Mom and Pops shrank down . . . down . . . down . . . and joined Little John inside the bottle.

"Uh-oh. Is there room for all of us?" Kaz asked, peering in at the other ghosts. The trip over had been pretty crowded. It would be even more crowded with two more ghosts in the bottle.

"Check the recycling bin." One of the solid men pointed at a large blue container in the corner of the room.

"There might be something in there that would hold all of you."

Claire walked over to the bin. She came back with a large jar. "How's this?" she asked.

"Much better," Kaz said. He and his grandparents shrank down . . . down . . . down . . . and swam into the jar. It smelled like pickles. Mom, Pops, and Little John swam out of Claire's water bottle and into the jar, too.

"Come here, Cosmo!" Kaz said as he clapped his hands together. "Shrink, boy! Shrink!"

Cosmo shrank down . . . down . . . down . . . and joined his family inside the jar. Then Claire took them all to the library.

CHAPTER 4

A GREAT IDEA

Who do we have here?" Beckett asked when Claire walked into the library craft room with a jarful of ghosts.

Kaz and his family passed through the jar and expanded. Grandmom and Grandpop gazed up at the paper birds that dangled from the ceiling.

"Beckett, these are our grandparents," Kaz said. "Grandmom, Grandpop, this is Beckett."

Beckett froze when Kaz said *grandparents.*

"Hello," Grandmom said, turning to Beckett with a friendly smile.

"It's nice to meet you," Grandpop said, offering his hand.

Beckett took it. "It's, uh, nice to see you again," he said, not quite looking Grandpop in the eye.

"Again?" Grandpop seemed confused. "Have we met before?"

Mom wafted over. "Dad, this is *Beckett,*" she said. "You know, from our haunt in the country."

Haunt in the country?

Grandmom's smile disappeared.

"What haunt in the country?" Little John asked.

Grandpop yanked his hand from Beckett's. He turned angry eyes to Kaz

and Little John. "*This* is the ghost who was looking after you?"

"Why didn't you tell us?" Grandmom expanded in front of them.

Kaz and Little John glanced at each other. "Tell you what?" Kaz asked. He and Little John had told their grandparents all about Beckett.

"We didn't know *this* was the Beckett you were talking about," Grandmom said.

"We can't stay here," Grandpop told Claire. "I demand that you take us back to Valley View at once."

"No, no," Beckett said, raising the palm of his hand. "I'll go."

"You were here first," Mom said. "We'll go." She motioned for Kaz and Little John to swim back into the jar.

"What? No!" Kaz and Little John protested.

"There are six of you. Seven, including the dog," Beckett said. "And only one of me. I can find a new haunt." He wafted over to Claire. "Would you mind transporting me to another haunt? Preferably one with some books?"

Claire shook her head. "I'm not taking anyone anywhere right now!" she said. "It's dinnertime. And I don't think my parents will let me go out again after dinner. So, unless you all want to blow around in the wind outside, you're stuck here until I get home from school tomorrow."

The ghosts stared at Claire.

"Tomorrow then," Grandpop said firmly. "Tomorrow you'll take us back to the nursing home as soon as you return from school."

* * * * * * * * * * * * * * *

"It's not fair," Little John moaned later that night while Claire and her family were asleep. "I don't want to live at Valley View with all the old people."

"Neither do I," Kaz said. "I don't know why we can't all live here together. What happened at the haunt in the country? Why are Mom and Grandmom and Grandpop so mad at Beckett?"

"I don't know," Little John said. "I think someone should tell us."

Kaz agreed.

But Pops couldn't answer any of their questions because he didn't know. And Mom, Grandmom, and Grandpop gave them the same answer: "It doesn't concern you."

It does too concern us if we have to leave the library, Kaz thought.

If no one else was going to tell them what happened, Kaz and Little John

thought they'd ask Beckett. But they couldn't find him. They searched upstairs, downstairs, and in the secret room. Beckett was nowhere to be found.

"Did he leave?" Little John asked as he and Kaz drifted around the secret room.

"How could he have?" Kaz asked. "Claire's asleep."

"Maybe he didn't go with Claire," Little John said. He snatched a ghostly shoe that hovered in midair.

Kaz and Little John were pretty sure that shoe belonged to their big brother, Finn. Finn had spent a few days at the library before Kaz had arrived. But then for some reason he went back into the Outside and no one had seen him since.

"Maybe Beckett went into the Outside like Finn and the wind blew him away," Little John said.

Kaz shook his head. "Beckett wouldn't do that," he said. "He's got to be hiding somewhere in the library."

And that gave Kaz an idea.

* * * * * * * * * * * * * * * *

In the morning, Kaz and Little John floated above Claire while she packed her backpack for school.

"What if Mom and Pops can't find us when it's time to go to Valley View?" Kaz

asked. "If they can't find us, they can't make us go to Valley View."

"You want to play hide-and-seek with Mom and Pops?" Little John asked.

"Sort of," Kaz said. "But I want to hide someplace where Mom and Grandmom and Grandpop can't find us. Maybe someplace that's not in the library."

"You mean you want to run away from home?" Claire said.

"Yes!" Kaz said. Then he thought for a second. "Wait. Maybe that's not such a great idea."

"Yes, it is!" Little John said. "It's the best, best, BEST idea!"

"We could get in trouble," Kaz said.

"Not if we're not here," Little John said. "Claire, will you help us run away from home?"

"Okay," Claire said. "I'll take you to

my school! You can hide there. I'll sneak you out the back door right now. When I get home this afternoon, I'll tell your family you're safe, but that you're not coming back until they say you don't have to go to Valley View."

"Great idea! Let's go!" Little John said as he shrank down . . . down . . . down . . . and swam inside the water bottle that was lying on Claire's bed.

Kaz hovered above the bottle while Claire zipped her backpack and lifted it to her shoulder. "Are you coming, Kaz?" she asked as she grabbed her bottle.

"Well . . . ," Kaz said. As long as Claire told everyone that he and Little John were safe, maybe it would be okay. "Yes, I'm coming!" He shrank down . . . down . . . down . . . and swam inside the bottle.

Claire headed for the back stairs. "See

you this afternoon," she called to her parents and Grandma Karen as she fast-walked past them.

"Wait, Claire," Grandma Karen said. "Why are you taking the back stairs?"

Claire stopped. She turned to her grandma and shrugged. "I just feel like it."

All of a sudden, Kaz and Little John's mom, pops, grandmom, and grandpop passed through the floor behind Grandma Karen.

"Uh-oh," Kaz said. He shrank a little smaller inside Claire's bottle.

Mom expanded to twice her normal size. "Where are you boys going?" she asked over Grandma Karen's shoulder.

"We're running away from home," Little John said. "And we're not coming back until you say we can stay at the library. Run, Claire. Run!"

"Bye!" Claire waved to her family and the ghosts. Hugging the bottle to her chest, she turned and tore down the back stairs.

"Oh no you don't. Come back here!" Grandpop plowed through Grandma Karen.

The grown-up ghosts raced after Claire. But Claire was faster than they were. She leaped over the bottom two steps and ran down a narrow hallway that ran behind the fiction room, all the way to the door at the end of the hall.

Kaz hardly dared to breathe.

"Hurry, Claire!" Little John shouted. The other ghosts were gaining on them.

Claire didn't slow down until she was out the door and safely in the backyard.

"Yay! We made it!" Little John cried as Claire slammed the door behind them.

Mom, Pops, Grandmom, and Grandpop hovered around the tiny window in the back door. Grandpop shook his fist.

Kaz moaned. "We're going to be in so much trouble when we come back."

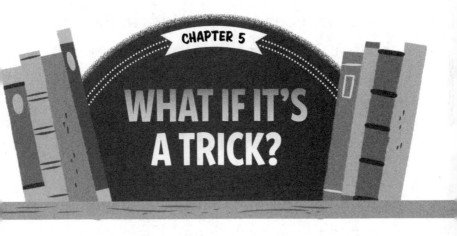

CHAPTER 5

WHAT IF IT'S A TRICK?

li waited for Claire under the big oak tree outside their school. "There you are!" he said, falling into step with her. He carried a book under his arm.

"Here I am," Claire said.

Kaz and Little John watched and listened from inside Claire's water bottle.

"I'm not grounded anymore," Eli said. He opened the door and they went in the school. "Can you come over this afternoon and find the ghost at my house?"

Claire dodged several kids in the hallway. "Your mom and your sister think *you're* the ghost," she said. "They said you don't want to move, so you're trying to make people think your house is haunted."

"But I'm not!" Eli said.

Claire spun the dial on her locker and opened the door. Kaz and Little John passed through the water bottle and floated up above Claire and Eli's heads.

Eli leaned against the locker next to Claire's. "I'll pay you if you can find the ghost," he said.

Claire wiggled out of her jacket and hung it in her locker.

"Don't do it, Claire," Kaz said. He dropped down in front of her. "Please, don't go over to his house."

"Why don't you want Claire to go to Eli's house?" Little John asked Kaz.

"Because I don't trust him," Kaz replied. "What if Eli plays a trick on her? We won't be there to help her. We're not going home with her after school, remember? We're staying here until Mom says we don't have to go to Valley View."

"We don't *have* to stay here. We could go to Eli's house with Claire," Little John said. "If he plays a trick on her, we could play a trick on him. Like this." Little John grabbed the book right out of Eli's hands, then let it fall to the floor.

Claire tried to hide her smile as Eli bent to pick up his book. He didn't even know why he'd dropped it.

"We can stay at his house tonight and then come to school with him inside his backpack tomorrow," Little John said.

"Well . . . ," Kaz said. There was no reason they couldn't do that.

"Earth to Claire," Eli said, waving his hand in front of Claire's face. "Will you come over after school or not?"

Claire closed her locker. "Okay, I'll come," she said. "But this better not be a trick!"

"It's not," Eli said with a grin. "I promise."

* * * * * * * * * * * * * * *

While Claire went about her school day, Kaz and Little John hung out behind the stage in the school cafetorium. The last time Kaz was back here was when he and Claire had solved the case of the ghost backstage. That was before he'd found any of his family except for Cosmo.

"I like your idea of us playing a trick on Eli if he plays a trick on Claire," Kaz told Little John. "But what kind of trick could we play on him?"

Little John shrugged. "He wants people to think his house is haunted. We could haunt *him*. We could glow and wail at him. You could transform some of his stuff. Then when anyone else comes into the room, we won't do anything."

"If only I *could* glow," Kaz said.

"You can. You did it at Valley View," Little John pointed out.

"Yeah, but I don't know how I did it," Kaz said.

"Well, there's no one around," Little John said. "Why don't you practice?"

Kaz looked at his arms. He looked at his legs. *Glow*, he told his body. *Glow! Glow! Glow!* He clenched his teeth and squeezed his fists.

Nothing happened.

Kaz sighed. While he was trying to figure out what else to try, Little John *expaaaaanded* really big in front of Kaz and screamed in his face, "BOO!"

Kaz almost jumped out of his skin. "What did you do that for?" he asked.

"I was trying to scare you," Little John said. "I thought maybe you glowed at Valley View because Petey had scared you."

"I don't think that's it," Kaz said, rubbing his arms. He wasn't glowing at all.

"Okay, relax," Little John said.

"How am I supposed to relax when you just scared me to death?" Kaz asked.

Little John swam behind Kaz and squeezed his shoulders. "Like this. Breathe . . . ," he said.

Kaz breathed.

"Breathe . . . ," Little John said again.

Kaz breathed some more. He could feel his body relaxing.

"Okay," Little John said as he swam in front of Kaz. "Now one more breath through your nose . . . and *glooooowwwwww*. Like this."

Kaz took one more breath and

61

watched as Little John started to glow. But he couldn't glow himself.

"I guess I'll do the glowing, and you can do the transforming," Little John said.

* * * * * * * * * * * * * * * *

"How are you going to find this ghost?" Eli asked Claire when they arrived at his house later that afternoon.

Kaz and Little John passed through Claire's water bottle and expanded.

"Do you have some special ghost-hunting equipment or something?" Eli asked.

"Yes. In here." Claire patted her bag.

"You should get it out," Eli said.

"I will if I need it," Claire said as she and Eli wandered from the kitchen to the living room. Kaz and Little John sailed above them. "Tell me again what's been

happening. You said you've seen this ghost."

"Yes. Lots of times," Eli said.

Claire was about to open a closed door off the living room, but Eli stopped her. "No, don't go in there," he said. "That's my mom's office. She's working."

Kaz tipped his head toward the door. *Is that* really *Eli's mom's office?* he wondered.

Or is there something in there that Eli doesn't want Claire to see?

"What are you doing?" Little John asked.

"Listening for clues," Kaz replied. "I told you, Eli plays tricks on people. Maybe this is the room where he keeps all his tricks."

"We don't have to listen out here," Little John said. "Let's go see what's in there." He passed through the door.

Kaz passed through, too, and the ghosts found themselves in a small room. Eli's mom was working at a computer in there.

"Looks like Eli was telling the truth," Little John said.

"I guess so," Kaz said as a phone on the desk jingled.

"Hello?" Eli's mom said into the phone.

"Let's go," Kaz said, turning around. He and Little John passed back through the

closed door and went to find Claire and Eli upstairs.

"I don't know what happens when people come to look at our house," Eli was telling Claire as they wandered into a bathroom. "We're never here when that happens. But the other people's real estate agent always tells our real estate agent that they saw a ghost. And then they don't want to buy our house."

"And that makes you happy," Claire said as she wandered around the room.

Eli shrugged. "It doesn't make me *un*happy. What makes me unhappy is getting blamed for something I'm not doing. And I'm not haunting my own house. I'm really not."

Kaz stared hard at Eli. He wished he knew whether Eli was telling the truth or not.

All of a sudden, there was a loud clatter behind Claire. Claire's ghost glass was lying on the floor.

"That's weird," Claire said as she bent to pick it up. "This was in my backpack. How did it fall out?"

Eli bit his lip. "I think the ghost pulled it out of your backpack," he said nervously. "It's probably hiding in the shower right now."

They both stared at the pink curtain that hung over the shower. Claire slowly reached over and pushed the curtain to one side.

There was nothing behind it.

"Eli?" his mom called from downstairs.

Eli, Claire, and the ghosts all went out into the hallway. "Yeah?" Eli said, leaning over the railing.

"That was another real estate agent

on the phone," his mom said. "We have to leave. He's bringing some people to look at the house."

Eli groaned. "Now?"

"Yes, now. Come on," his mom said.

Claire waited for Eli to start down the stairs, then whispered to Kaz and Little John, "See what you can find out while everyone's away."

"Okay," Kaz said. "See you tomorrow?"

"See you tomorrow," she promised.

CHAPTER 6

THE GHOST AT ELI'S HOUSE

Kaz and Little John swam into a girl's bedroom and peered out the front window. They saw Claire and Eli standing in the driveway with Eli's mom. It looked like Eli's mom was offering Claire a ride, but they couldn't hear through the closed window.

Claire lifted her backpack to her shoulder, and with a quick wave to Eli, she set off down the street. Eli and his mom got into their car and drove away.

Now Kaz and Little John were alone in Eli's house.

Maybe.

"Hello? Is anyone else here?" Kaz gazed around the bedroom.

"Come out, come out, wherever you are!" Little John called.

The ghosts heard a strange popping, dropping sound. It was coming from somewhere below them.

"What is that?" Kaz asked.

"I don't know," Little John said. "It sort of sounds like . . . popcorn."

"No. It sounds like . . ." Kaz thought for a second.

"Like what?" Little John pressed.

"I don't know," Kaz said. "Not popcorn, though. The pops are too slow."

The ghosts wafted out into the upstairs hallway.

"Hello?" Kaz called again. "Is anyone there?"

Pop . . . pop . . . pop . . . pop . . . pop . . .

Kaz noticed a desk over by the stairs. The top drawer was open. "Hey, was that drawer open a few minutes ago?" Kaz asked Little John.

"I don't know. I don't think so," Little John replied.

They swam over and peered down at the open drawer. There wasn't anything very interesting inside, just some paper, envelopes, pencils, and pens.

The popping stopped.

The ghosts drifted down to the main floor and saw a bunch of marbles lying all over the front hallway.

"Those were definitely not here before," Little John said.

"Was that what made the popping sound?" Kaz asked. He dove down and picked up a solid marble. Then, holding the marble carefully between his thumb and first finger, he carried it over to the stairs and let it fall. It bounced down the bottom three steps with a *pop . . . pop . . . pop* sound.

"It's the same sound," Little John said. "But no one's home, so who dropped all these marbles down the stairs?"

Kaz had a bad feeling about this, a very bad feeling.

Click! The front door lock turned. "I think you'll really like this home," a man with a briefcase said as he opened the door and came into the house. He was probably the real estate agent. A well-dressed man and woman stepped in behind him.

Kaz and Little John swam backward, away from the open door.

"It's well maintained and this is a lovely neighborhood," the real estate agent added. He set his briefcase down and closed the door.

"Oh!" the woman cried out as she slipped on a marble. "Be careful. There are marbles all over the floor!"

"I see that," the agent said. He hurried around the room and picked up all the marbles. He dropped them into a decorative bowl on a table and smiled uneasily at the couple. "Perhaps we

didn't give the family enough notice that we were coming. Let me show you the living room."

Kaz and Little John followed the group into the living room.

"Notice the beautiful stonework around the fireplace." The real estate agent tapped the stones.

"Wooooooooooooo!" Something inside the fireplace wailed.

The woman gasped. "What was that?" she asked.

"Probably the wind," her husband said, patting her hand.

Kaz and Little John raised their eyebrows at each other. It didn't sound much like wind to either of them.

"Hello?" Little John said to the beautiful stonework. Then he and Kaz swam into the fireplace and looked up

toward the chimney. They didn't feel any wind. And they didn't see anything that could have made that *wooooooooooooo* sound, either.

By the time Kaz and Little John returned to the living room, the solid people had moved on to the kitchen. The ghosts hurried after them.

"These are state-of-the-art appliances," the real estate agent said.

While the man and woman checked out the stove and refrigerator, another *pop . . . pop . . . pop . . .* sound came from the front hallway.

"What is that?" the man asked.

Kaz and Little John followed the sound. Now there were *more* marbles on the entryway floor.

The real estate agent walked right through Kaz and looked around. "I see

I missed a few marbles," he said as he gathered them up and added them to the small pile in the bowl.

But Kaz and Little John were pretty sure he had picked up all the marbles before.

Pop . . . pop . . . pop . . . A single marble rolled down the stairs. All by itself.

"Where are those marbles coming from? Is someone home?" the woman asked.

Kaz and Little John passed through the ceiling to the second floor. There was no one in the upstairs hallway, but the ghosts noticed something else. The desk drawer that was open a few minutes ago was now closed.

Who closed it?

The real estate agent and the man and woman were just arriving at the top

of the stairs. Kaz and Little John darted out of their way, into the first bedroom. It was Eli's room, according to the sign on the door. There was a large can of marbles sitting in the corner of the room.

"This is probably where the marbles came from," Kaz said as he floated past the can.

"Look! There's a book on Eli's bed," Little John said.

The book was open to Chapter 10: "How to Make People Think Your House Is Haunted." Suggestion number one was roll marbles down the stairs.

"This is the master bedroom," the real estate agent said as he led the man and woman into the bedroom across the hall.

A couple of seconds later, the man and woman ran out of the room SCREAMING.

Kaz and Little John swam over to see what all the fuss was about.

"I—I'm sorry," the agent called to the couple as he walked through Little John. "I don't know what's going on around here."

Kaz and Little John quickly poked their heads into Eli's parents' bedroom. They didn't see anything unusual, so they followed the solid people downstairs.

"This house is haunted!" the woman exclaimed as she yanked open the front door.

Kaz grabbed Little John's arm and swam backward so they wouldn't be blown into the Outside.

"We're not buying a haunted house," the man told the real estate agent.

The agent followed the couple outside, slamming the front door behind him. Kaz and Little John moved to the front window and watched the solids get into a brown car and drive away.

As soon as the car was gone, Kaz heard footsteps behind him. He turned to see Eli's sister, Lauren, walking into the living room from the kitchen.

Where did she come from?

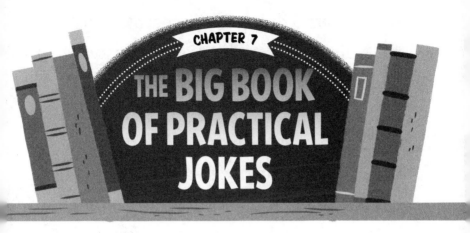

Lauren hurried up the stairs.

"Is *she* the ghost?" Little John asked.

"I don't know. I don't think so," Kaz said.

"I think she is," Little John said. "Otherwise, why is she here when everyone else is gone?"

"Maybe she just got home," Kaz suggested.

"Or maybe she's been here all along. Maybe she was hiding, and maybe she's

the one who dropped the marbles down the stairs and scared those people away," Little John said.

Kaz frowned. "Why would she do that?"

"Same reason Eli would," Little John said. "Maybe she doesn't want to move. Or maybe she wants everyone to think Eli's the ghost. She could be playing a trick on him because he plays tricks on everyone else."

"Could be," Kaz said. But he thought it was more likely that Eli was the ghost.

A little while later, the front door opened, and Eli and his mom walked in. Eli's mom was talking on her cell phone. "Yes, I understand," she said, closing the door behind her.

Eli started to walk away, but his mom held him by the elbow. "I will have a talk with him," she said into the phone. "Thanks

for letting me know." She set the phone on the table with the bowl of marbles. "Marbles on the stairs this time?" she said as she grabbed a handful of marbles from the bowl. "This behavior has to stop, Eli. Someone could have gotten hurt."

"I didn't do it!" Eli said.

Lauren came partway down the stairs. "Didn't do what?" she asked, resting her chin on the railing.

"Oh, I didn't know you were home, Lauren," her mother said.

"I just got home," Lauren said. "Cheerleading practice was canceled today."

"The ghost was here again," Eli told Lauren. "It rolled marbles down the stairs and scared away the people who came to look at our house."

"There's no such thing as ghosts," Eli's mom said in a tired voice.

Lauren turned and ran back up the stairs.

"Well, I know I didn't do it. I wasn't even here," Eli said.

Lauren returned a couple of seconds later with a heavy book. "Look what I found on Eli's bed," she said, tromping down the stairs. She marked a page with her finger and held the book so her mom could read the title: *The Big Book of Practical Jokes*.

"What were you doing in my room?" Eli cried.

"You borrowed my markers yesterday. I went to get them back," Lauren said. She turned to their mother. "Look what page the book was open to." She opened the book and read out loud, "'How to Make People Think Your House Is Haunted. Number one, roll marbles down the stairs.'"

"Eli!" their mom cried, hands on her hips.

"What?" Eli said. "That book was on my shelf when we left. It wasn't on my bed."

"It *was* on your bed," Lauren argued.

Kaz and Little John looked at each other. They'd seen the book on Eli's bed, too. But they didn't know whether it was there when Eli and Claire were looking around upstairs or whether it had appeared after they left.

"I wasn't here when any of that stuff happened," Eli said again.

"You could have rigged up something to go off when you're not here," Lauren said. "You like to play tricks on people. You know you do!"

Kaz knew it, too. He had seen Eli borrow books on the subject from the library.

"I'm being framed!" Eli insisted.

"Someone's trying to make it look like I'm the one doing all this stuff."

Lauren snorted. "Who would do that?"

"A ghost," Eli said. "I'm being framed by a ghost."

Little John shook his head. "I think you're being framed by your sister."

* * * * * * * * * * * * * * * *

Later that night, Kaz and Little John saw Eli pick up his phone and make a call.

"Hi, Claire?" he said. "It's me. Eli."

Little John's eyes widened. "He's talking to *Claire*!"

Kaz put his finger to his lips. He wanted to hear what Eli said to Claire.

"The ghost came back when those people were looking at our house," Eli told Claire. "It dropped a bunch of marbles down the stairs. Then it sort of

appeared in the lady's face and she got scared and ran away."

So that *was what happened in Eli's parents' bedroom.*

Eli switched the phone to his other hand. "My mom still thinks it's me," he said.

"It's . . . not . . . you . . . ," Little John wailed. *"It's . . . your . . . sister . . ."*

Eli jumped so high, he almost dropped the phone. "Who said that?" he cried.

"Little John!" Kaz glared at his brother.

"What?" Little John asked Kaz. "I'm just trying to help."

"That was the ghost," Eli hissed into the phone. "Did you hear it? It said, 'It's not you. It's your sister.'" He glanced nervously around the room.

Kaz swam over and put his cheek next to Eli's. He heard Claire say to Eli,

"No, I didn't hear it. Let's be quiet and see if it says anything else."

"Claire? It's me," Kaz said into the phone. He was careful to talk and not wail. He wanted Claire to hear him, but he didn't want Eli to hear him. "That was Little John who said 'It's not you. It's your sister.' We followed those people around the house. We didn't see the ghost, but Eli's sister was either in the house when those people were here or she came in right afterward. Little John thinks she's the ghost, but I don't know. I still think it's Eli."

"It's not," Little John argued.

Eli sighed. "I don't hear that ghost now," he said. "Big surprise. It never shows up when I need it to."

"Should I glow?" Little John asked Kaz.

"NO!" Kaz said.

"I can tell it's still here, though," Eli said into the phone.

"How can you tell?" Claire asked.

Eli shivered. "Because it's really cold in here," he said. "Do you think you could come over and find it now?"

"Sorry. I have to go to bed soon," Claire said. "But I'll come over tomorrow after school."

"Okay," Eli said with disappointment.

"See you tomorrow." He hung up and plugged in his phone. Then he scurried downstairs.

* * * * * * * * * * * * * *

"What do you think Lauren is doing?" Little John asked Kaz a few minutes later. The ghosts hovered above Eli and his parents, who were watching TV in the family room. Lauren was up in her bedroom.

"I don't know," Kaz said. He was much more interested in the TV show than he was in Lauren.

"She could be planning her next trick," Little John said. "Maybe I should go keep an eye on her."

"I'll stay with Eli," Kaz said. "Then if either Eli *or* Lauren does something suspicious, we'll know about it."

Little John swam away, and Kaz watched the rest of the TV show with Eli and his parents. When it was over, Eli's mom yawned and stretched. "Time for bed, Eli," she said.

Eli slumped down on the sofa. "Do I have to?" he asked.

"Yes," his dad replied. "It's late."

"Are you guys going to bed, too?" Eli asked.

"Soon," his mom said. "We're going to watch the news first."

"Can I watch the news with you?" Eli asked.

"No. It's past your bedtime." Eli's dad pointed toward the stairs.

"I don't want to be up there all alone," Eli said in a small voice.

"Your sister's up there," his mom said.

Eli rolled his eyes. "That's like being alone," he grumbled.

"What's the matter, Eli?" His mom ruffled his hair. "I know you're not afraid of the dark."

"No," Eli said. "But I'm kind of afraid of ghosts."

"There's no such things as ghosts!" Eli's dad said.

"Ding . . . dong . . . you're . . . wrong . . . ," a ghostly voice wailed from the kitchen.

CHAPTER 8

READY OR NOT, HERE I COME!

t's the ghost," Eli said, pulling his knees to his chest.

His mom scowled. His dad glared.

"What? Why are you looking at me like that?" Eli asked, his eyes shifting from one parent to the other. "I'm not doing anything!"

His parents got up from the sofa and headed for the kitchen.

"Wait for me," Eli said, running after them. Kaz followed close behind.

Lauren and Little John were already in the kitchen. Little John shrugged at Kaz as Lauren went from cupboard to cupboard, opening and closing doors.

"What are you doing, Lauren?" her mom asked.

"Looking for the recorder," Lauren said.

"What recorder?" her mom asked.

"The recorder that he hid in here." Lauren tilted her head toward Eli. "Didn't you guys hear that weird voice?"

Eli stomped his foot. "I didn't hide any recorder!" he said.

"Yes, you did," Lauren insisted. "And I'm going to find it and prove that you're the ghost once and for all."

"Maybe *you're* the ghost!" Eli shot back. "You were in here when that voice started talking."

"I was getting a snack," Lauren said.

"You probably rigged something up to go off when I opened the refrigerator."

"I didn't!" Eli argued.

"Did you see what happened?" Kaz asked Little John.

"Not really," Little John said. "I followed Lauren down here. And I heard the voice, too. It was right behind me. But when I turned around, there was nothing there."

"There's a cabinet behind you." Kaz pointed.

"I know. I looked in there, but I didn't see anything," Little John said.

Eli and Lauren's mom opened the refrigerator door. "I don't see any of Eli's

contraptions in here," she said, peering at the shelves.

"That's because there *aren't* any contraptions in there," Eli said. "I'm telling you, it's a ghost. A real, live ghost!"

"It did sound like a real ghost wailing," Little John said.

Kaz had to agree that it did. But he'd heard wailing like that before when he and Claire had been out solving other cases. And each time there was another explanation.

Lauren and her parents opened every cupboard and pulled out every drawer in the whole kitchen while Eli stood in the middle of the kitchen with his arms crossed.

"See?" Eli said when they finished. "No recorder."

"*Woooooooooo!*" Something wailed in the living room this time.

Everyone rushed to the living room. Nothing seemed to be out of place. There were no ghosts. No hidden recorders. Nothing.

"I don't know what's going on around here," their dad said. "But it's time for bed. For real this time."

"What about the ghost?" Eli asked.

"There's no such thing as ghosts," his dad said.

His mom nodded. "We're all scaring ourselves silly. Things will look better in the morning."

* * * * * * * * * * * * *

"I wish Claire was here," Kaz moaned

once Eli and his family were asleep. He and Little John wafted back and forth along the upstairs hallway. Kaz had no idea how they were going to solve this case.

"Claire's good at solving mysteries," Little John said. "But so are we. We can figure out what's going on ourselves."

"How?" Kaz asked.

"I don't know," Little John said. "We need a plan."

They'd already searched the house from top to bottom.

They'd tried splitting up. Kaz had kept an eye on Eli, and Little John had kept an eye on Lauren.

Kaz didn't know what else to try. "About all we can do is wait for something else to happen," he said.

"Maybe we can *make* something else happen," Little John said. "If it's a real

ghost, maybe we can figure out a way to make it come out."

"How?" Kaz asked again.

"Well," Little John said as he and Kaz reached the end of the hallway. They turned around and drifted back the other way. "If a new ghost came into the library, what could it do to make you or me come out?"

"It could say, 'Hi! Are there any other ghosts in this place?'" Kaz said. But they'd already tried calling out to any real ghosts in Eli's house.

"Eli said the ghost likes to play hide-and-seek," Little John said. "Maybe *we* should hide and see if we can make the ghost find *us*!"

"Sure," Kaz said. *Like that will actually work.*

Little John cupped his hands around his mouth and called out, "Do you hear that,

you ghost? We're going to play hide-and-seek. This time, it's your turn to find us!"

Kaz rolled his eyes. Only a real ghost would have heard Little John. And Kaz didn't think it was a real ghost. It was *never* a real ghost.

But right at that very moment, a ghostly shoe shot through the floor right between Kaz and Little John. And a voice they both recognized called out, "Okay. Ready or not, here I come!"

CHAPTER 9

FOUND!

s that . . . ?" Little John stared at the
ghostly shoe that floated in front of him.

Kaz grabbed the shoe and turned
it all around. "It sure looks like Finn's
shoe," he said. The voice sounded like
Finn's, too.

"Finn?" Kaz called. "Are you here?"

A ghost boy's head popped through the
floor in front of Kaz. "I thought you wanted
to play hide-and-seek," the boy said as he
rose through the floor. "But you're not even

hiding. Got you!" He tagged Kaz. "Got you, too!" He tagged Little John.

Kaz and Little John gaped at their big brother. It really *was* him!

"You're the ghost at Eli's house?" Little John said, not quite believing it.

"Yes," Finn said.

"You're the one who dropped the marbles down the stairs?" Kaz said. "You're the one who left that book on Eli's bed and made everyone think Eli was trying to scare people away? And you're the one who kept appearing and disappearing in front of Eli?"

"Yes. Yes. And yes!" Finn said.

"Why?" Kaz asked. "And why didn't you let us know you were here? You must have known *we* were here. We've been here for hours!"

"I wanted to see if you could figure it out," Finn said with a shrug. "I thought you were a big-shot detective now."

Kaz narrowed his eyes. "How do you know I'm a detective?" he asked.

"A few months ago, I heard Eli talking about a girl detective who finds and catches ghosts," Finn said. "Then I saw

a girl go into that house next door. I knew she was the detective because I recognized her from when I was in the library. That is one weird solid girl!"

"Claire's not weird," Little John said. "She's nice."

Finn snorted. "Any solid who can see ghosts when they're not glowing is weird!" He took his shoe from Kaz and plopped it on his right foot. There was no shoe on his left foot.

"Anyway," Finn went on. "I saw you floating outside the house next door a couple of months ago. That girl, Claire, was chasing you and calling your name. I figured you were working together. I've been trying to get Eli to call your detective agency forever! I had to glow *a lot* before he finally believed I was a ghost and not his imagination."

"Why did you only glow around him and around people who want to buy this house?" Kaz asked. "Why didn't you let the rest of his family see you, too?"

"I thought that if he was the only one in the family who saw me, *and* he was getting blamed for things I was doing, then maybe he'd finally call you guys," Finn explained. "But he never did. Not until he saw that girl walk by his house the other day."

"Hey, I think I saw you float across the window," Kaz said, remembering the ghostly whatever-it-was he saw for just a second. "Cosmo probably saw you, too. I bet that's why he was going crazy. Did you see us inside Claire's water bottle?"

"Her water bottle?" Finn said. "What were you doing in there? And why are

you guys hanging out with a solid girl, anyway? Why aren't you at the old schoolhouse?"

There was no quick answer to that.

Kaz took a deep breath. "We better start at the beginning," he said. He and Little John told Finn what all had happened since he had passed through the wall and blown away from the old schoolhouse. They told him about the old schoolhouse getting torn down—

"Wait. What?" Finn cried. "The old schoolhouse isn't there anymore?"

Kaz and Little John shook their heads. Then they told Finn about how the rest of the family had gotten separated, too. Little John told about the ghosts he met in the purple house. Kaz told about meeting Claire, and how they'd formed C & K Ghost Detectives, and how none

of their cases had led to real ghosts. But still, somehow, they'd managed to find Cosmo, Little John, Grandmom and Grandpop, Mom and Pops, and now him.

"Wow. That's amazing," Finn said.

"So, where have you been all this time?" Little John asked Finn.

"Well," Finn began. "First I rode the wind with Grandmom and Grandpop. They stayed together because they were holding hands, but I got separated from them when the wind blew me into a house.

There was a solid dog there that kept jumping up, trying to eat me, so I didn't stay very long. I went back into the Outside and then the wind blew me to the library. But I didn't want to stay *there*. Not with a solid girl who could see me when I wasn't glowing."

"You left your other shoe there," Little John said, pointing at Finn's stockinged foot.

"I know," Finn said. "My foot hurt because that solid dog kept biting it. So I took it off. I forgot to put it back on when I left the library."

"Where did you go after that?" Kaz asked.

"To a movie theater," Finn said. "I liked it there. There were other ghosts there. Like this ghost girl, Jessie. She was really cute. And this ghost guy, Dave. He

was old, like Mom and Pops, but guess what? He passed through a wall and got separated from his family when he was a kid, too! We kind of bonded over that. Plus we both liked to wail at the solids who came to see the scary movies."

"Why did you leave if you liked it there so much?" Little John asked.

"I didn't mean to. I sort of accidentally passed through the wall," Finn said.

Kaz shook his head. "You never learn."

"Hey, I didn't know that was an Outside wall!" Finn said. "And I do too learn! I haven't blown away from this haunt yet!"

* * * * * * * * * * * * * *

Later that afternoon, the front door opened, and Eli and Claire walked in.

"Claire!" Kaz exclaimed. He and Little John had been waiting all day for Eli and Claire to return. They had decided not to go to school with Eli that morning because they wanted to hang out with Finn. And because Claire had told Eli that she'd come over after school to find the ghost.

"Guess what?" Little John said to Claire. "We found the ghost at Eli's house. It's our brother, Finn!"

Finn raised his hand in greeting.

Claire nodded slightly. She couldn't really talk to the ghosts. Not in front of Eli.

"I don't know where that ghost is right now—" Eli began.

"Over . . . here . . . ," Little John wailed. His whole body started to glow, and he waved at Eli.

Eli's eyes opened wide.

"Little John!" Kaz exclaimed.

"Th-that's not the same ghost I've been seeing," Eli told Claire as he backed away from Little John.

Finn started to glow, too. *"Don't . . . worry . . . I'm . . . here . . . too . . . ,"* he wailed.

Eli's eyes opened wider. "Oh no!" he cried. "We've got *two* ghosts!"

"You guys!" Kaz said, shaking his head. "Why are you trying to scare that boy?"

Little John and Finn stopped glowing.

"Eli wanted Claire to come over and catch a ghost," Little John said. "She should pretend to catch us."

"She can do that without you glowing," Kaz said.

"Where'd those ghosts go?" Eli muttered as he looked all around.

Claire opened her backpack and pulled out her ghost glass and ghost catcher. "I see them," she said, peering through her ghost glass at Finn.

Finn stuck out his tongue and waved his fingers at Claire.

"You better get out of the way, Finn," Kaz warned as Claire raised her ghost catcher.

"Why?" Finn asked.

Claire pressed the button on her ghost catcher and it roared to life.

WWOOOO!!!

"AHHH!" Finn cried out. He swam backward and pressed his hands to his ears as Claire aimed her ghost catcher at a spot away from all the ghosts. "WHAT *IS* THAT?"

"IT'S CLAIRE'S GHOST CATCHER!" Kaz had to yell to be heard over it. "SHE USES IT TO MAKE SOLID PEOPLE THINK SHE CAN CATCH GHOSTS."

"SHE *COULD* CATCH US WITH THAT IF SHE WANTED TO," Little John said.

"I THINK YOU'RE RIGHT," Kaz said
as Finn hovered between him and Claire.

Finally, Claire turned that awful
machine off. "Got 'em," she said to Eli.
"Both your ghosts are in here." She
tapped the side of her ghost catcher.

"He doesn't really believe that, does
he?" Finn asked. He swam over and took
a closer look at Claire's foil-wrapped
"ghost catcher."

Eli looked doubtful. "Are you sure?"
he asked.

"I'm sure," Claire said firmly. She shoved her ghost catcher back inside her backpack. "If you have any more problems, give me a call. But I don't think you will."

"Okay," Eli said.

"Ha-ha-ha-ha!" Finn laughed. "He *does* believe it!"

Claire raised her water bottle to the ghosts and wiggled her eyebrows.

"Are you thirsty, Claire?" Eli asked. "Do you want to fill your water bottle?"

Claire smiled uneasily. "No. I'm good, thanks," she said, dropping her empty water bottle to her side. She wiggled her eyebrows at Kaz again.

"Oh! I think Claire wants us to go with her," Kaz said, swimming over to her.

"Go where?" Finn asked.

"Did our parents say we could stay at the library?" Little John asked.

Claire didn't answer. She just moved closer to the front door.

"We can talk to Claire once we're Outside," Kaz said as he shrank down . . . down . . . down . . . and swam into the water bottle. Little John swam in behind him.

"Come on, Finn!" Little John called from inside the bottle.

"You're coming with us, aren't you?" Kaz asked.

Finn shrugged. "I guess," he said. He shrank down . . . down . . . down . . . and swam into the bottle with his brothers.

CHAPTER 10

MOM'S STORY

Did Mom and Grandmom and Grandpop say we could stay at the library?" Little John asked Claire as soon as they were outside Eli's house.

"Are Grandmom and Grandpop still there? Or did they go back to Valley View?" Kaz asked.

"What about Beckett?" Little John asked. "Have you seen Beckett? We couldn't find him before we left."

"Why don't you guys let the girl talk instead of asking so many questions," Finn said.

Claire raised her water bottle to her eye level so she could talk to the ghosts while she walked down the street. "Thanks, Finn," she said. "Okay, here's what happened. I came home from school yesterday and

your parents and grandparents were really mad. They crowded around me and wanted to know where you were and when you were coming back."

"What did you say?" Kaz asked.

"I told them you were safe and that you weren't coming back until they said you could stay at the library," Claire said. "Then your mom was all, 'children don't make the rules.'" She copied Mom's voice.

Kaz gulped. "On a scale of one to ten, how much trouble are we in?"

"That's the thing," Claire said as she crossed the street. "I don't think you are in trouble. After they talked to me, your mom and your grandparents had a big talk with Beckett—"

"So Beckett *is* still at the library?" Little John interrupted.

"Yes," Claire said. "I wouldn't say everything's peachy between Beckett and your family, but things are better. They all want you to come home, so they made a deal. Beckett is going to live in the library. Your grandma and grandpa are going to go back to Valley View. But you and your parents are going to live *above* the library. Where my family lives. You don't have to go to Valley View. And you can visit Beckett whenever you want."

"Hooray! We don't have to go to Valley View." Little John clapped his hands.

Kaz wasn't ready to celebrate just yet. Just because their parents had said he and Little John didn't have to go to Valley View didn't mean they weren't in trouble. But maybe when their parents

saw Finn, they'd forget all about whatever trouble Kaz and Little John were in. And they'd all live happily ever after.

* * * * * * * * * * * * * *

"There you are!" Kaz and Little John's mom said when Claire walked into her living room. The ghosts passed through the water bottle and started to expand.

"Don't you ever—" Mom stopped midsentence.

She blinked, then rubbed her eyes and blinked again. "Finn?" she said. She turned to Claire and Kaz and Little John. "You found Finn?"

"MICHAEL! MOM! POPS!" Mom called. "YOU'LL NEVER GUESS WHO'S HERE!" She threw her arms around Finn.

"Oh my goodness," Grandmom said as she and the rest of the family wafted

into the room. They raced toward Finn, hugging and kissing him.

Woof! Woof! Cosmo barked.

Finn *expaaaaanded* over his family's heads. "Cosmo? Is that you?"

His tail wagging, the ghost dog worked his way toward Finn and started licking him all over.

Finn laughed. "I haven't seen you in so long, old buddy!" he said, hugging his dog.

"Thank you for finding Finn," Mom said to Claire.

"I didn't find him," Claire said. "Kaz and Little John did."

"Good thing we ran away from home, huh?" Little John said. "Otherwise, we wouldn't have found Finn."

Mom frowned. "Yes, we're going to talk about that."

* * * * * * * * * * * * * * * * *

"Don't you boys ever run away again!"
Pops said later, while Claire and her family
were asleep. Grandmom, Grandpop, Pops,
and Finn hovered nearby.

"Do you have any idea how worried
we were?" Mom added. "How could you
run away when we only just found each
other again?"

"We didn't want to live at Valley
View," Kaz said in a small voice.

"And you weren't listening to us,"
Little John said.

"Plus, we thought that if we had to
leave the library, you should at least tell
us why. What happened between you and
Beckett that was so bad we couldn't all
live here together?"

Mom glanced over at Grandmom and
Grandpop. Grandpop nodded slightly.

Mom turned back to Kaz and Little John. She took a deep breath, then said, "Okay, I'll tell you."

Everyone gathered around Mom, and she began her story. "Beckett and I knew each other because he used to live with us when we were kids."

"He did? Why?" Little John asked.

"Because he got separated from his own family. I'm not sure how or why. You'd have to ask him," Mom said.

That seems to happen to ghosts a lot, Kaz thought.

"Have you ever seen Beckett glow?" Mom asked.

"No," Kaz and Little John said at the same time. Kaz added, "He told me he hasn't glowed in, like, twenty years."

Mom looked a little surprised at first. Then she said, "That may be because of

what happened when we were kids. You see, when Beckett glows, he doesn't glow blue like we do. He glows red."

"He does?" Little John said, wide-eyed.

"Cool!" Finn said.

"No, Finn." Mom shook her head. "It's not cool. It's not cool at all. You see, I used to have a brother. He would've been your uncle Dave. He was just a young ghost when Beckett lived with us. He'd never seen Beckett glow before. None of us had. But one day Beckett glowed . . . and it scared my brother so bad that he jumped right through the Outside wall and blew away. We never saw him again."

Grandpop cleared his throat. "We asked Beckett to leave after that," he said. "We were so upset to lose our only son."

"And that's what happened," Mom

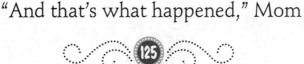

said, wiping a tear from her eye. "Seeing Beckett again after all these years brought back all those sad memories. I know it was an accident. But I still lost my brother, because of Beckett."

Neither Kaz nor Little John knew what to say. They just felt bad, for Mom *and* for Beckett.

"Wait a minute," Finn said. "What did you say your brother's name was?"

"Dave," Mom replied.

"I met a ghost named Dave at the movie theater," Finn said. "I wonder if he could be your brother."

Kaz could hardly believe it. Just when he thought he'd found his *whole* family, he learned about a brand-new family member.

"Oh, I don't know. There are probably lots of ghosts named Dave," Mom said.

"Still. It's worth checking out," Kaz said. What if Finn's friend Dave really *was* Mom's long-lost brother?

"Let's ask Claire to take us to the movie theater tomorrow!" Little John said.

"Yeah, let's!" Kaz said.

The ghosts could hardly wait for Claire to wake up.